W9-BRP-565

Trinity School
4886 Ilchester Rd.
Ellicott City MD 21043

Lucky Ducklings

By EVA MOORE • Pictures by NANCY CARPENTER

Orchard Books | New York | An Imprint of Scholastic Inc.

This is a true story about a mama duck and her five ducklings.
The rescue happened in June 2000 in the town of Montauk, New York,
on the end of Long Island. The people who helped the lucky ducklings are
Joe Lenahan, Paul Greenwood, Dennis Sisco, and Perry Aaland.
Shortly after this incident, the town replaced the storm drain grate with one
that has narrower openings that are safe for future duckling crossings.

Text copyright © 2013 by Eva Moore
Illustrations copyright © 2013 by Nancy Carpenter

All rights reserved. Published by Orchard Books, an imprint of Scholastic Inc.,
Publishers since 1920. ORCHARD BOOKS and design are registered trademarks of
Watts Publishing Group, Ltd., used under license. SCHOLASTIC and associated
logos are trademarks and/or registered trademarks of Scholastic Inc.

No part of this publication may be reproduced, stored in a retrieval system, or
transmitted in any form or by any means, electronic, mechanical, photocopying,
recording, or otherwise, without written permission of the publisher. For
information regarding permission, write to Orchard Books, Scholastic Inc.,
Permissions Department, 557 Broadway, New York, NY 10012.

LIBRARY OF CONGRESS CATALOGING-IN-PUBLICATION DATA
Moore, Eva.
Lucky ducklings / by Eva Moore ; illustrations by Nancy Carpenter. — 1st ed.   p. cm.
Summary: While following their mother through town, five little ducklings fall into a storm drain.
ISBN 978-0-439-44861-1 (hardcover : alk. paper)
[1. Ducks—Fiction. 2. Animals—Infancy—Fiction. 3. Rescues—Fiction.]
I. Carpenter, Nancy, ill. II. Title.
PZ7.M7835Sto 2012   [E]—dc23   2012002444

10 9 8 7 6 5 4 3 2 1   13 14 15 16 17
Printed in Singapore 46
First edition, February 2013

The display type was set in Omnibus Bold Italic.
The text was set in 18 point Omnibus.
The art was created using charcoal and digital media.
Designed by David Saylor

To the dedicated men and women of the Montauk Fire Department

and to volunteers everywhere.

— E. M.

For my sister, whose first word was "Quack!"

— N. C.

The Duck family

lived in a pretty pond in a green, green park, in a sunlit little town at the end of a long, long island.

Early one morning, Mama Duck swam to shore.
She hopped out onto the grass. Right behind her came

Pippin,

Bippin,

Tippin,

Dippin . . .

and last of all . . .
Little Joe.

What a fine day for a walk!
Off they went through the green, green
park. *"Whack-a-whack!"* Mama Duck
called to her brood. "Follow me!"

And Pippin, Bippin, Tippin, Dippin . . .
and last of all . . . Little Joe, lined up right
behind her. And off they went.

They came out of the park
and into the town.

The ducks had a bite to eat . . .

. . . then they went on their way.

Mama Duck went first.

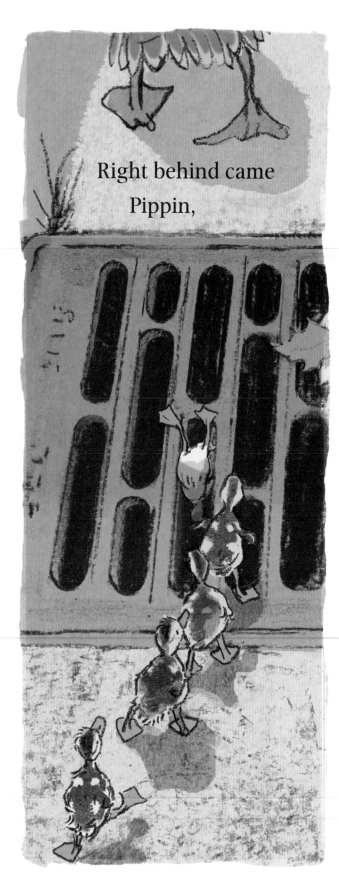

Right behind came
Pippin,

Bippin,

Tippin,

Dippin . . .

and last of all . . .
Little Joe.

Oh, dear!
That could have been
the end of the story.
But it wasn't, because . . .

Someone saw what happened.
"Help!" the woman cried.
"All the baby ducks fell into
the storm drain! Call the fire
department!"

People came to see what the matter was.
They could hear the ducklings making
a ruckus below.

Mama Duck heard them, too!
She ran back to the storm drain
and wouldn't let anyone get near.
"Whack! Whack!" she said.
"Get away from my babies!"

Quack!

Quack!

Quack!

Quack!

Quack!

Firemen Joe, Paul, and Dennis rushed
to the rescue. But they couldn't open the grate.
The ducklings were trapped!

Oh, dear!
That could have been the end of the story.
But it wasn't, because . . .

A man named Perry had an idea. There was a big roll of cable in his pickup truck. He hooked the end of the cable to the grate and then switched on the motor. The cable tugged on the grate . . .

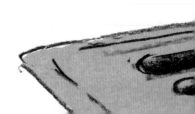

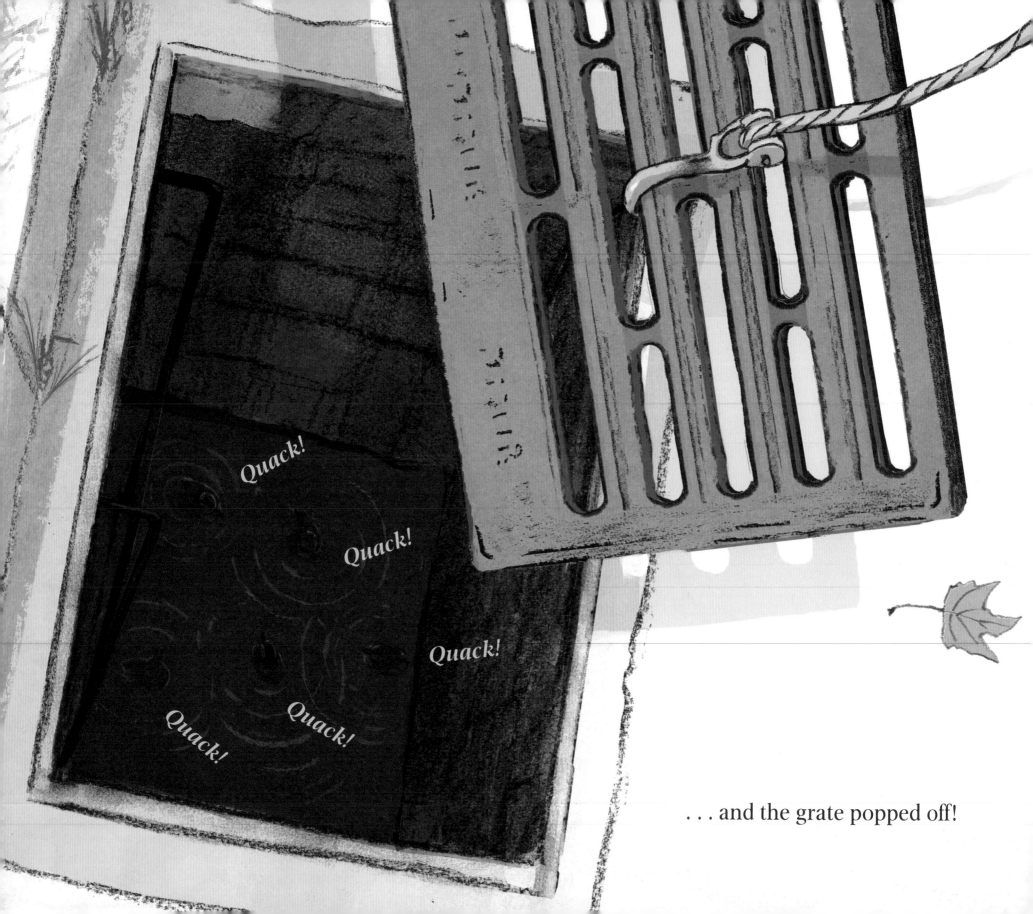

Quack!

Quack!

Quack!

Quack!

Quack!

. . . and the grate popped off!

Fireman Paul climbed
down,
down
into the storm drain.

Everyone waited . . .

. . . and when they saw

Pippin,

Bippin,

Tippin,

Dippin . . .

and last of all,
Little Joe . . .

. . . everyone cheered!

Fireman Joe picked up the bucket filled with ducklings and started to cross the road. He was going to take the ducklings back to the park.

Mama Duck came running after him.
"Whack! Whack! Whack!" she cried.
"Bring my babies back!"

Oh, dear!
That could have been
the end of the story.
But it wasn't, because . . .

Fireman Dennis knew just what to do.

Honk!
Honk!

Beep!
Beep!

At last, Mama Duck and her brood
were together again — all safe and sound.
"Whack! Whack!" Mama Duck said.
"What lucky ducklings you are!"
"Quack! Quack! Quack! Quack! Quack!"
her ducklings agreed.

The five lucky ducklings lined up behind their Mama, and off they went —

Pippin,

Bippin,

Tippin,

Dippin . . .

and last of all . . .
Little Joe.

And *that* is the end of the story.